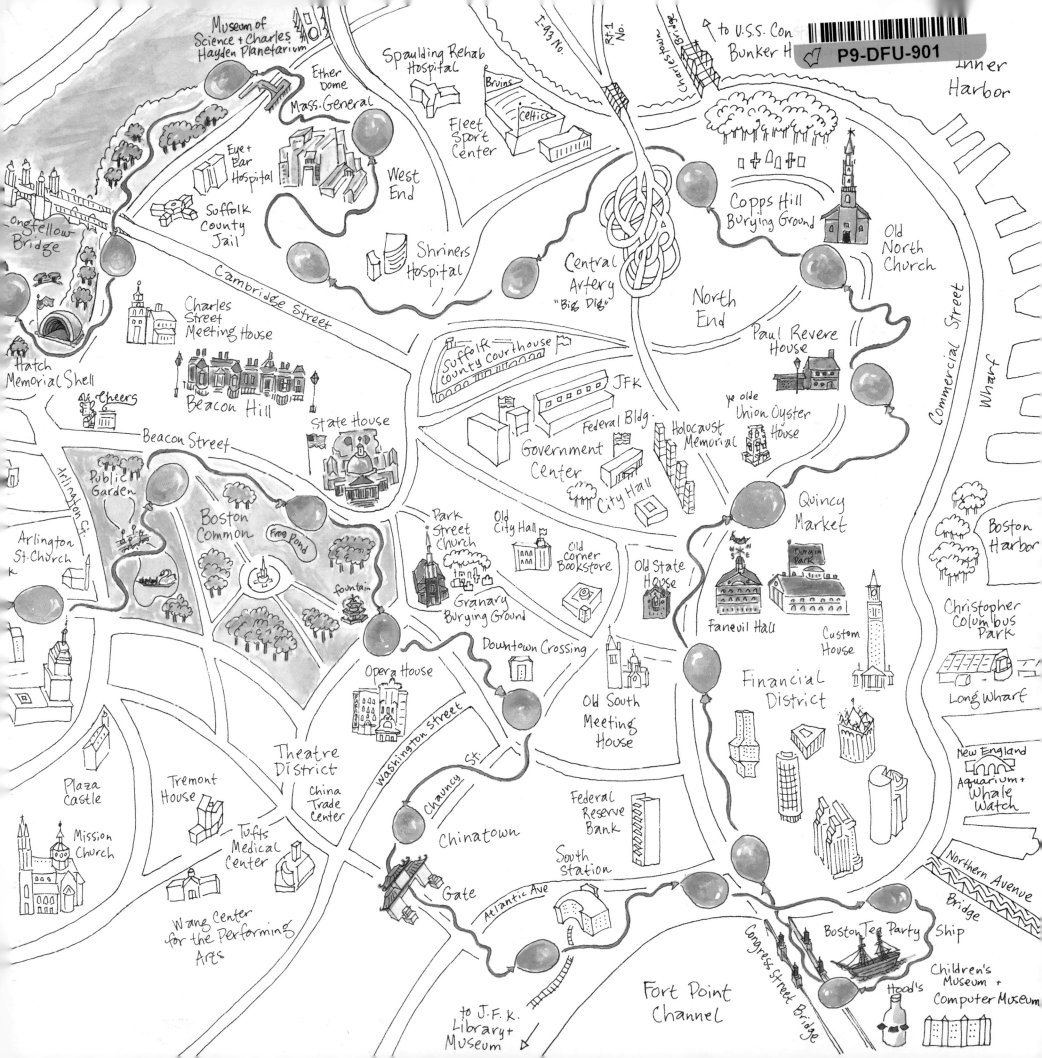

Dear Curran MaKaye
and
Tanner Payton,

May you find green balloons wherever you go ... and know that Aunt MaryKaye is watching over you.

Love,
Mim & G.P.
12/25/02

You Can't Take a Balloon Into The Museum of Fine Arts

story by Jacqueline Preiss Weitzman
pictures by Robin Preiss Glasser

Dial Books for Young Readers  New York

I would like to thank my husband, Larry, for all his support,
but like this book, there are no words.
—J.P.W.

For my children, Sasha and Benjamin—soar and fly!
—R.P.G.

Published by Dial Books for Young Readers
A division of Penguin Putnam Inc.
345 Hudson Street
New York, New York 10014

Copyright © 2002 by Jacqueline Preiss Weitzman and Robin Preiss Glasser
All rights reserved
Permission has been granted to have the title of this publication
read *You Can't Take a Balloon Into The Museum of Fine Arts*
Text set in Aunt Mildred
Printed in Hong Kong on acid-free paper
1 3 5 7 9 10 8 6 4 2

Library of Congress Cataloging-in-Publication Data
Weitzman, Jacqueline Preiss.
You can't take a balloon into the Museum of Fine Arts /
story by Jacqueline Preiss Weitzman ; pictures by Robin Preiss Glasser.
p. cm.
Summary: While a brother and sister, along with their grandparents, visit the
Museum of Fine Arts, the balloon they were not allowed to bring into the museum
floats around Boston, causing a series of mishaps at various tourist sites.
ISBN 0-8037-2570-1
[1. Boston (Mass.)—Fiction. 2. Museum of Fine Arts,
Boston—Fiction. 3. Balloons—Fiction. 4. Stories without words.]
I. Preiss-Glasser, Robin, ill. II. Title.
PZ7.W4481843 Yq 2002 [E]—dc21 2001028748

The artwork was prepared using black ink, watercolor washes,
gouache, and colored pencils.

MVSEVM OF FINE ARTS

JOHN SINGER SARGENT

CYRVS EDWIN DALLIN
AMERICAN 1861-1944
APPEAL TO THE GREAT SPIRIT
1909

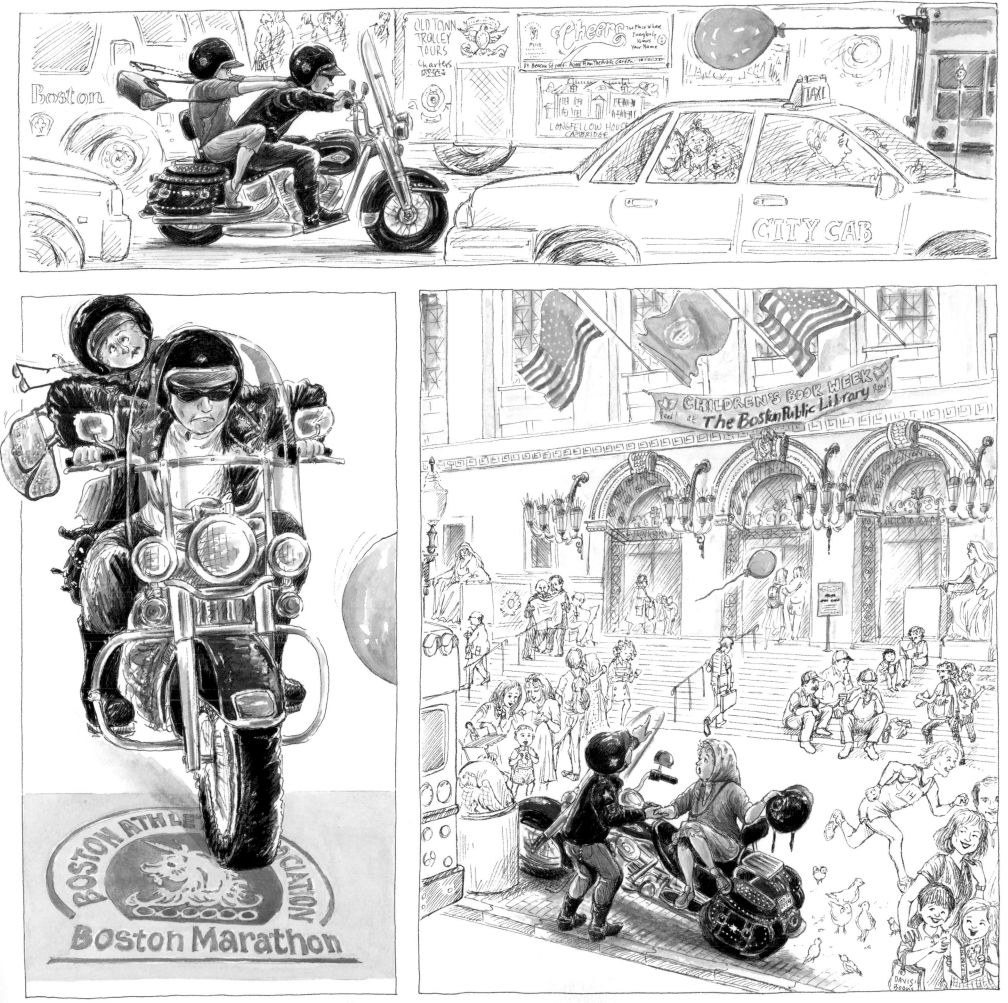

Acknowledgments

The author and artist would like to thank the following people for all of their help and support in making this book possible:

At the Museum of Fine Arts, Boston: Deborah Dluhy, Dean of The School of the Museum of Fine Arts, Boston, Deputy Director for Education; Christopher Atkins, Coordinator of External Media Licensing; David Sturtevant, Rights and Licensing; and Debra Lakind and Dan Reardon of MFA Enterprise.

In Boston: Carla Meyer, 39 Beacon Street; Shauna La Fauci and Joseph P. Mercurio, Boston University; Don Knuuttila and Tim Maguire, Boston Tea Party Ship & Museum; Seana Kelley and Thomas E. Ryan, Durgin-Park; Patrick Leehey, Paul Revere House; Carol Nashe, Boston Duck Tours; Stuart A. Rains, Citgo; Dick Bresciani, Vice-President of Public Affairs, and Kerri Walsh, Boston Red Sox; Michal Regunberg, Dr. Benjamin Davis, and Raymond Cyr.

At Dial Books for Young Readers: Toby Sherry, Editor; Atha Tehon, Art Director; Kimi Weart, Designer, Regina Castillo, Copy Chief.

We would also like to express our appreciation to our agent, Faith Hornby Hamlin; Nancy Spero; Sam Kunce and Jessica Reeves-Cohen, for Nancy Spero; Monica Marino, Artists Rights Society; as well as Marcia and Ralph Preiss, Dr. Ann Kaganoff, Stephen Garfein, Cari and Warren Abbate, and Satya Twena.

List of works of art reproduced from the collections of the Museum of Fine Arts

"The Appeal to the Great Spirit," 1909, (page 10), Modeled in Greater Boston, Massachusetts, cast in Paris, France, Cyrus E. Dallin, American (1861-1944), Bronze; Gift of Peter C. Brooks and others.

"Painter's Honeymoon," c. 1864, (page 13), Lord Leighton Frederick, British (1830-1896), Oil on canvas; Charles H. Bayley Picture and Painting Fund.

"Dance at Bougival," 1883, (page 14), Pierre Auguste Renoir, French (1841-1919), Oil on canvas; Picture Fund.

"Artist in His Studio," c. 1627-1628, (page 15), Harmensz van Rijn Rembrandt, Dutch (1606-1669), Oil on panel; Zoë Oliver Sherman Collection; Given in memory of Lillie Oliver Poor.

"Charles Sumner Bird and His Sister Edith Bird Bass," 1907, (page 17), Cecilia Beaux, American (1855-1942), Oil on canvas; Gift of Mrs. Charles Sumner Bird.

"Noonday Rest," 1866, (page 19), Jean-François Millet, French (1814-1875), Pastel and black conte crayon on paper; Gift of Quincy Adams Shaw through Quincy A. Shaw, Jr. and Mrs. Marian Shaw Haughton.

"Bato Kannon, the Horse-headed Bodhisattva of Compassion," (page 20), Japan, Heian period, twelfth century, Panel; ink, color, gold, and silver on silk; Fenollsa-Weld Collection.

"Drug Store," 1927, (page 21), Edward Hopper, American (1882-1967), Oil on canvas; Bequest of John T. Spaulding.

"U.S. Frigate Constitution," 1928, (page 23), J. Gregory Wiggins and W. F. Spicer, after M. L. Buschman, Red oak and other materials; Gift of J. Templeman Coolidge.

"Watson and the Shark," 1778, (page 24), John Singleton Copley, American (1738-1815), Oil on canvas; Gift of Mrs. George von Lengerke Meyer.

"Paul Revere," 1768, (page 26), John Singleton Copley, American (1738-1815), Oil on canvas; Gift of Joseph W. Revere, William B. Revere, and Edward H. R. Revere.

"Horse," (page 27), China, Tang dynasty, first half of the eighth century, Earthenware with three-color lead glaze; John Gardner Coolidge Collection.

"To the Revolution," 1983, (page 28), Nancy Spero, American (b. 1926), Unique print, printed by hand with collage on four sheets of handmade paper; Ernest Wadsworth Longfellow Fund.

"Lake Placid," 1919, (page 29), Florine Stettheimer, American (1871-1944), Oil on canvas; Gift of Miss Ettie Stettheimer.

"L'Enquêteur," 1973, (page 30), Jean Dubuffet, French (1901-1985), Epoxy, polyurethane, and paint; Gift of Charlotte and Irving Rabb. ©2001 Artists Rights Society (ARS), New York/ADAGP, Paris.

"Depart de Charles et Robert des Tuileries," December 1, 1783, (page 34), Antoine François Sergent-Marceau, French (1751-1847), Watercolor; Bequest of Forsyth Wickes, Forsyth Wickes Collection.

Faces from History

As we wandered through the winding streets of Boston, we were amazed at how often we came upon sights of extraordinary historical and social significance. Though many are being reused in modern ways, these places still evoke the memories of the daring men and women who influenced American life as we know it today. We enjoyed placing some of their images throughout the book. We hope you have just as much fun spotting them, and perhaps learning a little bit about their amazing accomplishments. —J.P.W. and R.P.G.

---

page 11: bottom right—on steps of the Boston Public Library, holding architectural plans
Henry Hobson Richardson (1838-1886) As the first American architect to achieve international acclaim, Richardson dominated American architecture in the 1870's and 1880's. He lived outside of Boston and his first major work was Trinity Church on Copley Square.

Charles Follen McKim (1847-1909) A partner in the highly acclaimed Beaux-Arts firm McKim, Meade and White, McKim was the designer of the Boston Public Library. He was a student of H. H. Richardson's, whose famous Trinity Church is located directly across Copley Square from the library.

page 11: bottom right—running past the group
William Henry Rodgers (b. 1947) Having won the Boston Marathon in 1975, 1978, 1979, and 1980, Rodgers became known as "Boston Billy." He was also a member of the 1976 U.S. Olympic Team.

page 15: top right—holding art supplies
John Singer Sargent (1856-1932) This expatriate artist was known for painting portraits of Boston's elite. He devoted the last years of his career to mural paintings, two of which can be viewed in Boston—at the Boston Public Library and in the Museum of Fine Arts, Boston.

page 16: bottom left—strolling in Boston Public Garden behind bench
Henry David Thoreau (1817-1862) This Massachusetts-born writer, philosopher, and naturalist is probably best known for his book *Walden*, a celebration of people living in harmony with nature, which records his observations while living alone for over two years on the shore of Walden Pond. It was Ralph Waldo Emerson who encouraged him to write.

Louisa May Alcott (1832-1888) This author of the beloved *Little Women* lived on Beacon Hill. She met weekly with Henry Wadsworth Longfellow, Henry David Thoreau, and Oliver Wendell Holmes at the Old Corner Bookstore on Washington Street.

page 17: bottom left panel—under the windows
Henry Wadsworth Longfellow (1807-1882): This author of such well-known poems as "Paul Revere's Ride" and "The Song of Hiawatha" was the most widely published and famous American poet of the 1800's. Longfellow married Frances "Fanny" Appleton in July 1842 on the second floor of 39 Beacon Street. They lived for eighteen years in Cambridge in an eighteenth-century mansion, now known as Longfellow House, that had served as George Washington's headquarters during the Revolutionary War.

page 18: top right—in front of the State House
Julia Ward Howe (1819-1910) This author and reformer was one of the most famous women of her time. She was very active in the anti-slavery movement and she wrote the words of "The Battle Hymn of the Republic," inspired by her visits to military camps during the Civil War. After the war, she wrote and lectured on women's rights and literacy, among other topics, and was the first woman elected to the American Academy of Arts and Letters.

page 18: top right—below dog walker
William Lloyd Garrison (1805-1879) One of the most important abolitionists in American history, he gave his first anti-slavery speech in Park Street Church in 1829.

page 18: bottom left panel—standing on corner
Marquis de Lafayette; Marie Joseph Paul Yves Roch Gilbert du Motier (1757-1834) Joining the American army at age twenty, this Frenchman served on Washington's staff and helped secure French support during the Revolutionary War. His headquarters was located on the corner of Park and Beacon streets.

page 18: bottom left panel—under relief sculpture
Robert Gould Shaw (1837-1863) Shaw led the African American Fifty-fourth Massachusetts Infantry in a fatal assault on Fort Wagner, South Carolina, on July 18, 1863. His story was depicted in the film *Glory*. The Robert Gould Shaw Memorial by the sculptor Augustus Saint-Gaudens, located across from the State House, is a stop on the Black Heritage Trail, which illustrates African Americans' contributions to early Boston history.

page 18: bottom right panel—walking by the trees
Elizabeth Vergoose (d. 1690) She is buried in Boston's Granary Burying Ground. Many believe her to be the legendary "Mother Goose."

page 19: top left—on walkway
Reverend William Blackstone (d. 1675) Boston's first settler, he sold the land that is now Boston Common to the city in 1634.

page 19: left corner of bottom right panel
Ralph Waldo Emerson (1803-1882) This Boston-born essayist, critic, poet, orator, and popular philosopher played a major role in influencing the thought and literature of American culture. He was often seen tending his mother's cow in Boston Common.

page 20: top right panel—under balloon
Phyllis Wheatley (1753-1784) Born in Africa and kidnapped at age seven, she was sold to a Boston family, who educated her. She became one of the best-known poets of her day.

page 23: on bridge—in eighteenth-century dress
Deborah Samson (1760-1827) Impersonating a man, Samson enlisted on July 20, 1782 as Robert Shurtleff in the Fourth Massachusetts Regiment of the Continental Army.